JUL 1 5 1993

# One Dog Day

# One Dog Day

## J. PATRICK LEWIS

illustrated by
MARCY DUNN RAMSEY

Atheneum 1993 New York

Maxwell Macmillan Canada
Toronto
Maxwell Macmillan International
New York  Oxford  Singapore  Sydney

Atheneum
Macmillan Publishing Company
866 Third Avenue
New York, NY 10022

Maxwell Macmillan Canada, Inc.
1200 Eglinton Avenue East
Suite 200
Don Mills, Ontario M3C 3N1

Macmillan Publishing Company is part of the Maxwell Communication
Group of Companies.

First edition

Printed in the United States of America

10  9  8  7  6  5  4  3  2  1

The text of this book is set in Goudy Old Style.
The illustrations are rendered in pen-and-ink wash.

Library of Congress Cataloging-in-Publication Data

Lewis, J. Patrick.
    One dog day / by J. Patrick Lewis; illustrated by
Marcy Ramsey.— 1st ed.
        p.      cm.
    Summary: With the help of her new friend Twef, twelve-year-old
Jilly and her dog Poetry win the annual coon dog race in Effingham.
    ISBN 0-689-31808-1
    [1. Dogs—Fiction.   2. Racing—Fiction.   3. Contests—Fiction.]
I. Ramsey, Marcy Dunn, ill.   II. Title.
PZ7.L5866Do      1993
[Fic]—dc20                                                    92-24573

To
ELIZABETH HEISNER

# One Dog Day

# 1

In Effingham in August, in the heat, in the heart of Illinois, on a wide pond fastened to a field, there was a contest folks waited all summer to see: The Third Annual Coon Dog Race and Corn Feed.

By the size of the crowd, you'd have guessed it was the county fair. More men and boys than cattails surrounded that pond, all bragging at once about the speed of the four-legged locomotives straining against their raw-hide leashes.

is what the barbershop sign read.

The scene was a blur of shirtless chests and overalls, brightly colored caps, and ears of corn roasting on open coals. There must have been enough chewing tobacco in that one place to plug a leak in Dickey's Dam. But most unusual of all were the dogs—close to a hundred of them—bluetick hounds, redbones, black and tans. They barked as if they were eating the wind, and the sound swelled up like a great howling of wolves.

The sun fell through cotton ball clouds and touched everyone who was there. The hot August breeze carried a message all its own with the sweet smell of buttery corn and cotton candy billowing out of the Farm Co-op concession trailer. Oh, it was a day. . . .

To an outsider, it must have looked like any dog could win this race. But in these parts, everyone knew a grudge match when he saw one.

Two years before, in the First Annual, a

3

gentleman farmer by the name of Abner Smalley embarrassed the rest of the field. His three dogs sailed across the pond like water spiders. It was more like a massacre than a contest.

Then the following year, Ned Durant, an upstart from two counties over, embarrassed Mr. Smalley. In the championship race, Durant's beagle edged out Smalley's dogs by a long nose. So most of the talk and all of the wagers settled on these two breeders and their champions.

By the time Smalley arrived in his orange-and-chrome van, the pond, which was half the size of a football field, was packed three or four people deep all around. Smalley tipped his cap to the crowd as he got out and ambled to the back of the van with the unmistakable stride of a winner. In a sea of tattered overalls, he alone was dressed in a fancy shirt, string tie, and pants pressed for Sunday.

Abner Smalley wanted no one to underestimate the pride and money he lavished on his dogs. He opened the back door and was greeted in a rush by his three roaring redbones. If they had been horses, you'd have thought they were Kentucky Derby thoroughbreds by the looks of them.

Over by the judge's table, devilment danced in Ned Durant's eyes. His hair shot out in all directions at once as if it were electrified. He was coat-hanger thin and strung tight as bailing wire, his cheeks gone hollow like he'd sucked a couple too many sour apples. He stood close by as Smalley paraded his dogs up to the judge.

Smalley wasted no time getting in the first lick. Laying a dollar down for each of his entries, he turned to the crowd so all could hear.

"My dogs's got papers goin' all the way back to the *Mayflower*. Their ancestors probably chased raccoons from one end of Europe to the other. Folks," he said, sweeping his arm in a grand gesture, "y'all are in for a real treat today!"

Durant laughed in a nervous, cocky way. "Papers don't win coon dog races, Abner. I guess you plumb forgot who whupped your pups last year, how my dog slid over this pond like a stick of oleo!"

He nudged his prize beagle, whose rubbery

5

sword of a tail whipped against the knees of the spectators standing near him, including Abner Smalley's.

The gentleman farmer didn't flinch.

"No, no, I ain't forgot last year," said Smalley. "Folks'll always recall a fluke, a freak accident. But sticks of oleo don't win coon dog races, Durant. A true winner's got the chase in his blood. That's why this is gonna be a redbone day."

That exchange set the crowd to buzzing, and the betting pace picked up plenty.

# 2

But the coon dog race was a social event, too, and the tension of the race was offset as farmers fanned themselves and took up old acquaintances, some they hadn't seen but once or twice since the Second Annual. Talk of the heat and hog prices and eggs mixed in with gossip about church picnics and taxes, the new post office in Effingham, and didn't they deserve a decent mayor sometime soon.

Along about one o'clock, the registration and tagging of the dogs almost completed, some commotion stirred up near the dock, across the pond from the judge's table. A button-sized, blond-haired twelve year old appeared in the loud line of farmers. She wore a red ruffled blouse, white shorts, and gym shoes.

Her name was Jilly and she stared down at the raccoon, pacing back and forth in his cage in the rowboat. Though she knew the animal was safe, she felt a little sorry for it.

The dog waiting silently beside her glanced at the raccoon but paid it no mind. This was no coon dog but a collie, and she was as out of place here as a bird in a beehive. The coonhounds growled at her but the collie looked ahead, calm and unafraid, the way collies will do, and stayed close to her small owner.

Heads turned as the crowd slowly came to notice the girl and her dog. Those around the dock began poking fun at the odd pair. In between bites on his corn on the cob, an old coon hunter said, "That animal's all over fur! She'll take to water like a stone."

Minding an old mutt with dozens of nicks on his ears and sides, a boy about Jilly's age spoke his piece, too. "Hey, girl," he said, "this here's a dog *race*. Ain't a dog *show!*"

A lean young man about twenty had as

much trouble holding his tongue as he did his feisty black and tan. "Young'un, I believe you'd best take that pretty thing back to the sheep ranch where you found her."

They had all got into the spirit of the thing when giant George Olsen waddled over to where Jilly, private in her thoughts, waited patiently for the race to begin. He had a thousand face-freckles that looked like they could burst into bloom any minute.

"What's your name, little lady?"

"Jilly. Jilly Hawkes," she said.

"Jilly Hawkes here!" he announced to the whole world. "Wearin' number thirty-three! Well, now, Jilly Hawkes, this critter of yours got a name?"

"Poetry," said Jilly, barely above a whisper.

"Pottery? How's that?"

"Poetry. Her name is Poetry."

"What kinda name is that—Poetry? Why didn't you just call her Table or Chair, or somethin' else dull?"

Farmer Olsen shaded his eyes and looked across the pond until he spotted Abner Smalley. "Looks like we got some real stiff competition for ya here, Mr. Smalley."

Among these jittery coon dogs, the collie hardly moved.

"*Stiff* competition, get it?" His own joke tickled him so that his rollicking laughter caused his undershirt to split halfway up the right side. Trying to hide his embarrassment, he teased, "Oh, but I can't wait to see slow Poetry in motion!"

Jilly took all the joking good-naturedly, for that was how most of it was meant. She nodded, smiled, and held on to the piece of cardboard with the number 33 on it she had received when she paid her one-dollar entry fee.

It was strange, Jilly had to admit, that she and her collie should be here in the thick of these lightning-fast dogs. Her father had farm business in Effingham and had driven down from Beecher City, her hometown, which was no bigger than a minute. He had tried to tell Jilly that a collie was no match for a coon dog, but she reckoned that Poetry could keep up with them in water even if she had never chased a raccoon. Anyhow, it was as tolerable a way to spend a Saturday as any she could think of. In Beecher City, she had all the time there was, and very little use to make of it.

# 3

Poetry laid herself down in the newly mown grass near the water's edge. Jilly sat down, too, and brushed through the dog's thick fur. The collie had been a present on her seventh birthday. She called her new puppy Hopeful then for reasons she could not remember.

About that time her mother began to read her stories and poems, especially poems, at bedtime. One poet in particular Jilly loved—Emily Dickinson—something like that. Hard words some, but she always seemed to understand the sound and sense of them.

They made a game of it. Her mother would

ask her to guess what the poet was thinking
with lines like

A NARROW FELLOW IN THE GRASS
OCCASIONALLY RIDES—

and she guessed snake right off. Before her
mother could finish the poem that began with

I LIKE TO SEE IT LAP THE MILES—
AND LICK THE VALLEYS UP—

Jilly said she bet Miss Dickinson must have
been thinking of a train when she wrote it,
and Jilly's mother fairly glowed with pride.

It was one of those poetry nights in
Beecher City that Hopeful, still a pup then,
lost her name and found a new one.

Jilly leaned back now, stopped petting the
dog, and said, "Hey, Hopeful." The collie had
forgotten. Her long tongue hung out as she
panted in the heat and gazed out at the pond,
so remarkably blue.

"Hey, Poetry," Jilly said, and Poetry
turned her head and laid her wet chin in the
girl's lap. Jilly took a couple of licorice jelly

14

beans out of the pocket of her shorts and let Poetry lap them up from her hand. "Oh, you are somethin', dog!" she laughed.

"Somethin's *right*, girl, but danged if I can say what it is." The low husky voice came from the woman next to Jilly. "People here sure are gonna get their money's worth today. What with a champeenship duel between Abner Smalley and Ned Durant "—she paused and hunkered down next to Poetry— "and a circus all in one."

The woman looked at Jilly. "I expect you got a tough enough hide to take all the funnin' they'll make of this queenie dog of yours?"

With a squinty sort of smile, backlit by the sun, Jilly edged a little closer to Poetry. "I expect," she replied.

# 4

The idea of the race was pretty simple. The dogs were to go off the dock in heats of six each, sixteen heats in all. On the judge's side of the pond, about fifty yards away, there was a twenty-foot pole stuck in the ground. A rope with a hook on the end dangled down.

Another rope was tied to the boat with the raccoon in it. Two men on the pole side would pull the boat across the pond, always keeping the raccoon out of harm's way, some yards ahead of the dogs, who would swim after it like the fever.

As soon as the boat got to the other side,

the men would grab the cage, hook it to the pole, and heave the raccoon, chittering away, in the air. A few seconds later, the dogs would come streaking out of the water toward the pole, yelping at the lonely critter in the cage, high out of reach.

A dog got points for "line"—swimming straightest and getting out of the water first—and points for "tree," if he was the first to run up to the pole and bark at the raccoon.

Now a black and tan can smell a raccoon a couple of hundred yards off. So you can imagine how frantic these hounds can be when the animal they're born to track is rattling his cage just a few yards in front of their wet noses. Poetry must have felt like a stranger among so many coon dogs—all of them born naturals.

Soon it came time for Poetry's heat, and Jilly led her out onto the rickety dock. She whispered final instructions in the dog's ear. Poetry seemed to be listening, stiff and silent as a statue, in a line with five other dogs barking and squirming all over the place.

The men on the far side began to pull the boat away. When the raccoon was out a safe distance, the judge fired his gun in the air.

The dock shuddered as the dogs flew off like diving birds. Well, four of them anyway. The wiry bluetick on the end got so wound up that he stumbled and fell in the shallow water. Another hound lit out sideways around the edge of the pond and hugged the shore all the way around.

Both dogs were disqualified.

Every face in the crowd was fixed on the water. For a single instant in Effingham in August, in the heat, in the heart of Illinois, no one spoke at all. Their mouths had dropped open in wonder, their words choked back in astonishment. For Poetry swam like a streak, like a dolphin far ahead of a trailing school of dogfish, and with each second she pulled farther away.

She had nearly caught up with the boat when the men yanked the cage and quickly hooked it to the pole. That didn't matter to Poetry. She rose out of the water, shook off her wet coat, and looked around to see where Jilly was.

The other dogs finally reached the bank and raced past Poetry to where the raccoon sat safely in its cage, high above the howls.

"Well, spit!" said George Olsen, still grabbing his split undershirt, "I don't believe this is happenin'!"

"Ain't happenin', George," someone replied. "It already happened! Why, your mutt looked like he was countin' fish when that motor-dog flew by."

Poetry got no points for tree because she didn't even notice the pole or the raccoon. But all those points for line put her in the final sixteen.

Jilly ran all the way around the pond to fetch her dog, the crowd, dumbstruck, watching her. She didn't gloat or whoop or snicker, but she couldn't disguise the pride she felt and she smiled as wide as the pale blue afternoon. The girl and her dog trotted off and lay down for a rest before the next round.

# 5

Nearly two hours later, after the first heats had eliminated all but the sixteen winners, the judge drew the dogs' names out of an old slouch hat to place them in the three semi-final races. Gentleman Smalley was slightly miffed when he learned that all three of his redbones had to compete against each other in the first race. But even this jot of bad luck couldn't dull his shine. He was sure he'd walk away the winner.

By now the excitement and the temperature had made a shambles of Ned Durant's electric hair, which drooped over his neck in

ringlets. Yet he sighed, secret and joyful, knowing his beagle could coast in the second race, not having to face Smalley's fearsome redbones.

And Poetry was to go up against three blue-tick hounds in the third race. In the eyes of most it was still all Smalley and Durant—no one else had a chance. Folks figured Poetry had got lucky in a heat with bum mutts. After all, what kind of creature was that to outswim a blue-ribbon coonhound?

By now a string of cars and pickup trucks ran for half a mile on either side of the dirt road that led to the pond. The losing hounds had either been taken away or slept in the shade of the trees, so their earlier howls now gave way to human noise, as the crowd swelled to twice what it was at the start.

Smalley didn't disappoint his fans. His redbones finished first, second, and third in the second race, and at the pole they looked as cool as long drinks of water. He led them back to his air-conditioned van, brushed them down, and pampered his winner, Roscoe Sunup, for the big race.

Jilly marveled at the sight of Smalley's

graceful dogs flying nose to nose across the pond. After Durant's beagle won the next race easily, Jilly jumped up and burrowed her way through the crowd toward the dock. Step for step, Poetry followed her as if on an invisible chain.

"Hope is the thing with feathers" was the line that kept running through Jilly's head. Who wrote that? she wondered. Edna St. Vincent Millay? Or Miss Dickinson? She couldn't remember. Maybe the poet meant that fear was the thing with feathers. It seemed like a whole pillowful had been let loose in her stomach. That or a bushel of butterflies, monarch-size.

Jilly needn't have worried. If that collie knew mercy, she didn't show it. At the crack of the gun, Poetry dove, while the blueticks walloped in the water. By the time the hounds surfaced, she led by five yards. Ninety seconds later, she waited, soaked through, on the winning side, the hounds still fighting the waves she had made.

Back on the dock Jilly was clapping and cheering. But again, no points for tree. Poetry hadn't barked once, but the judge knew what

everyone knew: The collie would face Smalley's redbone and Durant's beagle in the final race.

A bullhorn boomed out over the crowd. "We'll take a half-hour break," the judge announced. "Still got two hundred delicious roasting ears begging for teeth over there. Get 'em while they're hot!"

Jilly waited in line to buy two taffy apples. She and Poetry stretched out under a weeping willow, ten yards in back of the crowd. The taunts, even the good-natured ones, were gone now. Folks passing by gawked at Poetry and made their grudging compliments. Jilly nodded thank-yous all around.

The quiet of the willow tree was peaceful compared to the flurry bubbling up around the judge's table. All the experts gathered there, in a hurry to give advice.

Durant looked sick and said as much. "I never seen the likes. Here's a coon dog race and we gotta have a flyin' fool of a dog showin' everybody up. It's got me hangin' off the drop edge of yonder."

Voices of experience came back like buckshot.

"Beat her at her own game, Neddy. Get your beagle quick and low in the water. There's the trick."

"Collie's too big, she'll be tuckered out in the final."

"Yeah, and the girl over there's got the dog eatin' taffy apples. Reckon she'll bloat."

Abner Smalley left his dogs in the van and joined the philosophers. As usual, George Olsen spoke up. "You ain't said much, Abner. Whatsya thinkin'?"

"It's queer enough, all right," Smalley replied. "Two things you're forgettin', though. One, that collie hasn't gone stroke for stroke with my Roscoe Sunup. And two, I don't believe the dog's got a voice box. She hasn't barked yet, and even if she could, she couldn't tell a coon from a coyote!"

George Olsen spit a wad of tobacco in a long arc onto a lily pad and nearly sank it. "I heard *that!*" he said. "Gonna be some cinch finish. I know where the smart money'll be a-sittin'."

The sun crawled over some clouds and faded off a bit to the four o'clock side of the sky. Poetry had rolled over and slept peacefully. Jilly doubted that she could win this race, but there was something about being here, something in the trying, that made it seem right. That the two of them had come this far . . .

Her mother and father were going to be amazed when she brought home the ten-dollar third-place money.

# 6

It was then that she saw the boy walking toward her. He used a yard-long branch for a cane, though he had no limp at all. Behind him followed—well, wallowed would be more like it—a bulldog pup with puffy eyes and a pug nose.

The boy seemed to Jilly like the kind of person who enjoyed talking to himself. And indeed, just when he got a few yards away, she heard him mumbling something about doodlebugs on a fly rod. Suddenly he saw her and his face opened like a sunburst.

"It's you! You're the one, ain't you?" he

said, his voice pitching high and low, sometimes on the same word, in a magical kind of
way Jilly had never heard before.

"The one what?" she asked.

"The one what?! Why, the one who's got
these coon doggers rasslin' with their souls!
Mind if I join you?"

Before she could say she didn't mind in the
least, he plopped down on the other side of
Poetry. "Ouch!" he said. "Dang stickaburrs!"
His blue jeans were covered with them from
chasing his bull-pup around in the long grass.
He pulled the burrs off and gently threw them
in the direction of the dog, who was flat on
his back scratching himself.

"It's an honor and a pleasure," he said,
laying a hand on Poetry's side. "This here is
some fine speed queen. Where'd you get her?"

Jilly told him all about the birthday present
and Beecher City and Miss Dickinson.

"Poetry," he whispered, peach fuzz playing
around the corners of his mouth. "Take my
dog now. Why didn't I think of a neat name
like that for him?"

They glanced over at the bull-pup, who

could well have been the ugliest dog in Effingham on any day of a natural week.

"Truth to tell," he said, "he don't put you much in mind of a poem, does he? More like a boulder, I'd say. Maybe I shoulda called him Rock. Instead I call him Buzz. Hey, Buzz, meet Jilly here and Poetry."

Buzz got up and fell over again in the dirt as if he hated to give up that particular patch of land.

"He's a reg'lar genius, that one," said the boy. "But he's also the best-naturedest old fool Arkansas ever bred.

"Say," said the boy, "if you're wonderin' how I knew your name, it's 'cause I was standin' over by two-ton Olsen when he was joshin' you. Don't mind him, Jilly. Somehow he's managed to get dumber by the month. I remember last year he brought a watermelon to the race. When his dog lost in the first heat, lost bad, he sliced the melon down the middle, ate half, and strapped the other half to his dog's back. Then he went around the pond askin' who wanted a camel ride. Don't that beat all?"

"He didn't bother me," Jilly lied.

"Your Poetry taught him a lesson, but I don't expect he'll ever learn it."

Jilly pulled her knees up to her chin and looked sideways at the boy. "You didn't say what your name was."

"Good reason for that. It's not one I'm rightly proud of. Promise not to tell?"

"Cross my heart," said Jilly.

He took a breath and shut his eyes against the pain. "Fairborn Farley Garland. There, I said it. Don't feel much better about it either. Sounds like a name oughta have bells on it, don't it? They called me F. F. for a while I guess and then my pa took to callin' me Two-F and that became Twef and that's what I am. Twef Garland, and I'm stuck with it."

Jilly couldn't help but laugh at the way he described it, like some kind of torture.

"Knew I shouldn'ta told you," he said.

"It's fine, Twef. One of a kind. Where you from?" asked Jilly.

"Down Elmo way. We moved here from Arkansas a few years ago so's my pa could head up the granary in Effingham. Anyhow, my pa's real love is coon dogs, don't ask me why. Buzz and me, we just tag along. See that man in the plaid shirt over there at the table lookin' like a judge?"

Twef raised his hand and pointed through the legs of the spectators on the bank. Jilly looked down along his arm to see where he was pointing. "Right there," he said. "Mr. Durant's bent over with his nose in the man's face. I'll wager Durant's braggin' or cussin', one."

"Yeah, I see him," Jilly said. "Why, that *is* the judge."

"Yep. That's my pa. He organized this event short after we moved here and I can't tell you how popular he is 'cause of it. A whole year in the plannin', three years runnin'."

A breeze cool as tap water blew through the willows and cottonwoods. Twef closed his eyes, lifted his head, and smelled the corn-roasted air. "I'm not complainin'," he said. "Because you sure do meet some interestin' people." Then, without thinking, he gave Jilly a look you could pour over pancakes. Lucky for him she wasn't looking. He stuttered onto the subject of the race.

"F-five minutes to go before Poetry's up on

34

stage. Say, Jilly, this dog don't say much, does she?"

"Just her nature, Twef. She's not a watch-dog. Nothing much needs watching in Beecher City."

"Too bad. I was hopin' she'd yelp just once! It's gonna take line *and* tree to win this one. Oh, wouldn't these coon doggers roll over if she was to . . ."

Twef went quiet, thinking.

# 7

A festival of gnats swarmed in front of them. Jilly shooed them away. Her mind wandered off to Elmo, where she tried to imagine what days were like there for Twef. Once, she remembered, her mother had taken her and Poetry to Elmo to buy chicken feed. The only thing about that trip that came back to her now was colors, like a dozen other towns she'd been through, towns where brown, the color of deer, curled around whitewashed houses.

She wanted to ask Twef, "Isn't this something? Wouldn't you trade twelve birthdays and Halloween for this coon dog race?" Instead, she could only say, "Poetry's done right well for herself today. But I don't think she can win—"

"Hold it!" Twef blurted out. "Got an idea! Might work and it might not. Listen, Jilly, you don't know how this race works, but my pa— I mean, the judge—picks three men out of the crowd to set the dogs off. So you won't be able to be with the Poet dog here. With a million and three people flocked around this pond we won't even see the water unless we find a better spot."

The man assigned to Poetry came to fetch her. Jilly put her cheek next to the dog's face and held tight.

"Come on, Jilly. Let her go. She'll do fine," Twef gently prodded. Jilly got up and watched the man lead Poetry to the dock. Roscoe Sunup and Durant's beagle were already there, imitating runaway freight trains.

Behind the raccoon's pole, forty feet from the water's edge, there was a clearing that provided a wide view of the race. No one was standing there, and this was where Twef wanted to be.

Jilly took off her shoes and wriggled her

toes in the soft baked earth, as the crowd jostled for the best seats at the lip of the pond. Twef's father picked up the bullhorn and kindly asked those in front to sit down so that others could see.

"In number-one position, Roscoe Sunup, owned by Mr. Abner Smalley, Effingham." Smalley's redbone heard the applause, but a dog wired for speed needs no prompting.

George Olsen, having placed his bets, sat in a heap a few feet from the judge. His voice boomed across the pond. "Git up, Roscoe boy, you show 'em!" From the other side, someone—maybe a Durant fan—yelled back, "You're gonna lose the rest of your T-shirt on this race, Georgie boy!"

"Number two," the judge called out, "is Scooter, owned by Mr. Ned Durant, Hillsboro." More applause. Durant did a little jig, as Scooter kept his sleepy-sad eyes on the raccoon in the boat.

"And in third position, the surprise of the day"—Get on with it, Pa, Twef mumbled to himself—"we welcome Poetry, owned by Miss Jilly Hawkes, Beecher City."

Silence.

Four, five seconds of the awful quiet you expect for the dearly departed. Then Twef started clapping wildly, his arms going up and down like pump handles, as if the queen of England had arrived. Spectators swiveled their heads toward the clearing. The judge turned in his chair to see his son whooping and whistling. Twef? Who couldn't have cared less about coon dog races? What was he doing down there? But the judge stood up, happy to join in the welcome for Poetry.

And soon the pitch nearly matched that for the redbone and the beagle. Jilly blushed. "Stop, Twef," she giggled. But he wouldn't stop, and each clap sent a hundred goose bumps along her arms and legs. Even the die-hard coon doggers paid their respects to the furry outcast.

# 8

The judge finally interrupted. "Gentlemen, are you ready?" The three starters at the dock gave the okay, and the men at the pulley did the same. "Then pull the boat!"

Scooter and Roscoe Sunup howled to see the raccoon drifting away. Mr. Garland raised his gun and pulled the trigger.

*Whop!*

*Whoosh!*

The three dogs hit the water running and were lost to sight under the great cannonball splash. A movie Jilly had once seen flashed through her mind, of dogs in slow motion,

diving into a pool, the beauty of it, the grace—
a ballet.

For Poetry there would be no pulling away this time. She was in the race of her life and somehow she knew it.

At twenty yards out, they were even, churning furiously in the water, swimming straight as corn rows, when the pulley jammed! The coon chittered nervously in her cage as the boat lay idle on the pond.

One, two, three seconds! The sight of the helpless creature pumped the champion blood of the coon dogs and they pulled ahead. Roscoe Sunup came within a foot of touching the boat when the men, cursing on the pole side, rammed the pulley handle down hard. It caught and the rowboat jolted forward, nearly tilting the coon's cage overboard.

"Hurry, Poetry, hurry, girl!" Jilly was shouting, screaming. Twef, lathered in sweat and all-gone hoarse, whipped his left arm like a windmill, unaware that he had taken Jilly by the other hand. And all along the bank, there was a riot of pushing and pointing— prodding the dogs on.

At the halfway point, the redbone took a

short lead over the beagle, in front of the collie by a length. Back at the dock, the usually cool Abner Smalley became a jumping bean, while Ned Durant, knee deep in water, smacked at the surface, yelling, "Catch him, Scooter, catch him!"

Then for the first time, Poetry saw Jilly behind the pole, and her powerful front paws paddled faster and faster. As they neared the shallow water Poetry caught the coon dogs, and she passed them just as the men hooked the cage to the pole.

She touched land a full length in front of the other two. In one long, graceful motion, she came out of the water, and without break-ing stride, she flew over the sand and the mud toward Jilly, the other dogs a breath behind her.

Twef had taken a shiny black object from his pocket. When Poetry was five feet from the pole, he put the object to his mouth. Sud-denly, the collie stopped short! Just under the raccoon pole, she barked once, twice, then ran into Jilly's arms, the two of them rolling over and over in the clearing.

Twef fell flat on his back, dazed. "It

worked! It worked! I knew it would!" He rolled onto his stomach and elbows, his fists holding up his chin. "Hey, girl," he said again, "that sure is some fine speed queen!"

"Twef!" Jilly shouted, her clothes drenched from heavy wet fur. "She barked, oh how she barked! Poetry, you treed a coon!"

"The winner of the Third Annual Coon Dog Race and Corn Feed"—as if the judge had to explain it to the spectators—"Poetry, owner Miss Jilly Hawkes, fifty-dollar first prize!"

# 9

Chores or naps or supper might have beckoned folks home, but they all stood, hammerstruck to the ground, cheering for Poetry. All except Ned Durant, who had looked up at the sky and then, as if fainting, fallen backward into the pond. George Olsen was emptying his wallet for a dozen bad bets.

Abner Smalley came to fetch Roscoe Sunup, and tipped his cap to Jilly. "If there was a national coon dog race, Miss Jilly," he said, "I'd be right proud to enter that collie. She won this race fast and fair."

Twef squirmed a little but no one noticed.

The concession trailer began to pull away, and the crowd did, too, moving slowly down the dirt road to their cars. "Come on over here and claim your prize, young lady," said the judge, still surrounded by dumbfounded experts.

Neither Twef nor Jilly heard Mr. Garland at first. Shoes in her hand, Jilly was exhausted and leaned against the raccoon pole. She raised her right foot and rested it on the inside of her left knee. Twef never saw anyone stand that way before, but it seemed so soft and natural.

Then Jilly said, "How do you figure it, Twef? Poetry barking and all. I thought she might win the line, but the tree?"

Twef shuffled sideways and stuttered again. He thought about fibbing but he thought twice. Maybe it wasn't such a good idea to keep the secret from Jilly.

"Y-you see, it's like this. Buzz here is so short, why, he can't even see over sidewalks. Gets lost real easy. So I always carry this little gizmo."

He handed her the shiny black object—a silent dog whistle.

47

"It makes a high screechy sound us humans can't hear. When a dog hears it, well, it's like a fire alarm goin' off in her head, and she'll more'n likely bark. Nothin' illegal about it. Course, I don't expect anyone ever thought to outlaw it where coon dogs are concerned. They need a dog whistle like they need a second nose! But for some animals, I'd say you've got to correct for the unfair advantage. So I guess you took care of the runnin', I took care of the barkin', and Poetry did all the swimmin'. How's that for teamwork?"

Jilly thought about it carefully. "By next year's race, Twef, Poetry won't need any help. Or any correction either. By then I'll make sure she's a real coon dog in sheepdog's clothing!"

Jilly heard her father calling to her from the road and collected her fifty dollars—more money than she had ever held before. She thanked Mr. Garland, who was scratching Poetry gently under her chin.

"I do hope we'll be seeing you and this Poet dog next year, Jilly," said the judge.

"We'll be here sure," she said.

# 10

Watching the girl and the dog ramble slowly down the road, the old experts agreed that they knew from the first how much spunk that collie had.

Jilly took her time to let Twef catch up to her, finding excuses in the pebbles she skipped over the pond. For a while they walked together without speaking. Talk can sometimes take away the magic in things.

Twef nervously brushed his hair over and cleared his throat. "You gotta be here for the Fourth Annual, Jilly. You just gotta be! When news gets out about what happened here

today, there'll be twice, three times as many people, from all over the country!"

He jumped out in front of her and walked backward so he could see her face. "And so will I 'cause we're a team, remember? I'm kinda like the pit crew!"

"I wouldn't miss it for anything, Twef, not for anything."

The sky bloomed orange and deep blue. Evening gathered in the branches of trees. Little by little and much by much, Twef realized that this was the tag end of one perfect day.

And the beginning of one long year.

The owner shook hands with her pit crew, and walked on to meet her father.

Suddenly Twef had another idea, and he shouted after her. "I spend most Saturdays in Effingham with my pa, Jilly! If you get down this way, you can find me at the granary or at Martin's, the drugstore. Bring Poetry and we can do our plannin' for next year!"

Jilly looked back, waving and nodding at the same time.

"What's this I'm hearing about Poetry, Jilly?" Her father tousled her hair, put his arm around her shoulder, and opened the car door. "How in thunder did this collie of yours beat a bunch of down-home coon dogs in a coon dog race?"

Jilly climbed into the backseat with Poetry and was just about to tell him the whole wonderful story. About Twef, the redbones and the blueticks, fifty new dollars, line and tree. . .

TELL ALL THE TRUTH, BUT TELL IT SLANT.

Suddenly old Miss Dickinson was back, rooching around in her brain. She turned to see Twef through the rear window. Tossing Buzz in the air, he seemed deliriously happy. As happy as Jilly herself.

"I guess we just got lucky, Pa. Real lucky."

Then the car rumbled down the dirt road, and found the highway to Beecher City and to home.